DIARY WITH YOUR NAME

LAKHAN MAHAVIR AGRAWAL

"In the name of all those nights, Where I kept writing...
and she kept listening to someone else's talks."

For those silences, Who listened to me completely, but in
whose midst she never stayed. I read this book on the basis
of those eyes, Who never looked towards me... but who
wrote every story of my life. And most of all, in the name
of that girl.

" Who was in every line of mine... but never came till the
last line of my life. "

– Lakhan Agrawal

Contents

FOREWORD

Some stories are not written... they just happen. And some diaries... are not just for keeping secrets - they are written in someone's name, to fill the whole life.

I started writing this diary probably the day I saw her for the first time. Maybe her one smile cleared the way for me on every page. There is no cheesy love story in this book... it is a journey of those silent glances where saying "I love you" is not necessary - just its existence is enough.

Every page, every line, every word... was for him. Maybe it will remain for him. But this time, I did not write this diary just for myself...

I wrote it for all those people, who have ever wanted someone immensely... without getting anything.

If you have ever prayed for someone more than yourself... If you have ever felt your worthlessness in the words written in someone's name...

Then it is possible that this story is yours too.

This diary is not a record of my feelings.

This is the book of my life... every page of which was in his name.

- Lakhan Agrawal
The boy who wrote... and waited.

PREFACE

"Diary With Your Name" is not a story - it is a wait. A love that was not spoken, it was just written. Every moment is a memory where a person is searching for his own world in the eyes of another... without any hope. Writing this preface was the most difficult for me. Because in this book I have not just written words... I have written everything of mine. I wrote it for that girl... whom I only saw, understood, felt - but never got. This diary is for those people -

- Who never get to speak what is in their heart.
- Who live every day thinking of a name, but never get to touch that name.
- Who love silently... and just write.

I don't know if this book will become a bestseller or not. But if even a single heart feels this after reading it...
"Yes, this was my story too..."
Then every line written by me, every pain, every silence... will be worth it.
"This book is not just the voice of my heart...This is of all those hearts... which have just been giving a name for someone."
– Lakhan Agrawal
Writer of a love that never needed a reply.

Acknowledgements

First of all, thanks to the name...for which I wrote this diary.

Kritika – you were the purpose of my words. I never talked to you, but your silence made me write every line of mine. Then thanks to those two friends...

Jiya and Raju – who not only listened to my stories, but also walked with me in every emotion. You both not only understood me – you never let me break.

Jiya, your drama, your lines like fragrance, and your saying "Oyeee hero!" – every time my heart was pacified.

Raju, your filmy swag and your friendship that touched every corner of the world made me laugh when I was breaking down.

Without you both, Lakhan would have been just a boy who wrote... you kept me alive. I want to thank from my heart every reader...who has ever loved someone from the heart even without getting them.

And finally...

Thank you to that diary...which was not just a piece of paper for me – it was the truest secret of my life.

"I kept writing, she kept reading...And the world kept just watching and thinking."

– Lakhan Agrawal

PROLOGUE

Some loves... do not happen by saying them. They just happen in a glance. Without a sound... without ownership...They just stay in the eyes – forever.

I did not know her...But without her name, not even a single page of my diary has been written. I could not leave her...But without her thoughts, I could not live even for a day. This story is not for those people, Who walk holding hands in love...This is for those –

Who live their whole life for a single face even while standing far away. His smile was my morning. His silence was my night. And his name – the last word of my every prayer.

I could never become his...But my every line, every emotion, every eye – was his. This diary... is his name.

"This is not my story...This is written for her happiness. That is life, in which I was never present."

– Lakhan Agrawal

Writer of a name he never got to call his own.

I just kept writing

I was just writing, she was just readin. Some stories don't start... they just get written. This first part is from the same heart that wrote this - which never got to speak in front of her, but kept writing her name on every page. There was her smile in every word, noise of her memories in every silence.

This is not a story, it is a diary...A diary that was just written, sometimes read - but never understood. In which there was love, but no expression...There were hopes, but no rights...And the deepest thing?

She used to study daily, but still she never saw me. This is the first part of those unknown days - where just a glance changed life... but a name hidden behind that glance could never become a part of her life...

I

When the Heart Silently Fell at First Sight

Royal Glory International School. The name itself was enough. The classiest, most royal, and most premium school in all of Uttarakhand. Getting admission here was like receiving a golden ticket to a dream life. Designer bags, high-class attitudes, luxury cars, stylish crowds – everything was here. But the most special thing that day... was the entry of Lakhan Agrawal. That boy... it was hard to tell whether he was truly classy or if it was just the magic in his eyes.

A complete silent lover type... spoke less, impacted more.

Black premium watch, sharp haircut, royal school blazer, and those calm expressions – his entry went straight into hearts.

The way he walked... like a slow-motion scene from a movie.

Girls practically floated in the air just seeing him.

But the one he spoke to the most... was Jiya .

His childhood best friend. Full drama queen. Full of mischief. Over-expressive. And the boldest girl around.

After the assembly, she walked straight up to Lakhan with her coffee bottle – full on taunting mode.

Jiya :

"Hey Mr. Royal Attitude... you're looking extra handsome today... what's the deal, huh?"

Lakhan smiled with his eyes – his signature move.

Lakhan:

"The same old story, Jiya ... handling the world in silence."

Jiya rolled her eyes —

"Yeah yeah... you're writing a love story without dialogues, right?"

And then... his eyes landed on Kritika Patil.

Simple. Beautiful. Graceful.

White kurti. Light blue jeans. Ponytail. And in her eyes – a different kind of peace... a whole other level of elegance.

Jiya immediately dropped a line —

"OHHH... I get it now! So this whole handsome look is because of Madam Kritika's royal entry!"

Lakhan froze for a second...

Kritika, walking toward the classroom with her bestie Riya, laughing and talking...

And Lakhan... was just staring at her.

Capturing every moment of hers... with his eyes.

Jiya whispered softly —

"You're officially about to become One-Sided Lover of the Year!"

Lakhan, in a low voice —

"Tell me, Jiya ... does love really need a mic to announce itself?"

Jiya , still teasing —

"One day, you're gonna propose just through your eyes, I swear..."

But Lakhan's eyes... were still fixed on Kritika...

That girl... there was something different about her. A calmness... that the other stylish girls just didn't have.

Jiya bumped his shoulder —

"Go bro... go talk to her... or else it's gonna be an FIR for stalking!"

Lakhan gave a faint smile —

"Let the time come, Jiya ... at the right moment."

And just then, Kritika walked past them...

And for one moment... their eyes met.

Kritika gave a soft smile... looking straight into Lakhan's eyes...

And in that one moment... Lakhan's whole world stood still.

Jiya , shocked —

"Ooooo bro! Kritika smiled at you as a return gift!"

Lakhan, from the heart —

"That one moment... is enough for me to live a lifetime, Jiya ..."

As they entered the classroom...

Jiya leaned close to his ear and said —

"Royal Kritika of Royal Glory... and Royal Lakhan... bro, this love story is gonna be a blockbuster! "

Lakhan quietly took out his leather-bound diary...

And on the first page, he wrote:

"Kritika Patil..."

"The name... in which all my happiness is tied."

Just then... Principal Sir entered...

Principal:

"Lakhan Agrawal! Diary in class again? Come on, give a speech in front of everyone!"

The whole class started laughing...

Jiya , teasing in a low voice —

"Ooho bro... the Royal Lover got on the stage... let's see what you do now!"

Lakhan, with a calm face, walked toward the stage...

But in his eyes... There was only one name shining — Kritika Patil.

The entire hall was absolutely silent.

Lakhan stood on the stage... but his eyes were focused on just one person — Kritika Patil.

Standing in the front row with Riya... a gentle smile on her face, Kritika was looking at him...

She was thinking —

"How does this guy stay so calm? How can such simplicity have such an impact?"

And in that moment... Lakhan picked up the mic.

His voice... calm, yet capable of stirring hearts from within.

Lakhan (as 'Thought of the Day'):

"Style is important in life...But simplicity is the real attitude."

The whole hall... froze for a moment.

He paused and looked around... then spoke again —

Lakhan:

"People who talk too much are only trying to show off...But the real ones... speak everything with their eyes."

A second of silence... then the entire hall erupted in applause!

In complete shock, Jiya whispered —

"Oye hoye! Bro just dropped a full-on movie-level dialogue!"

But the most special thing?

Kritika's soft smile...

She was looking only at Lakhan... and in her eyes, there was a unique kind of admiration... a real emotion.

For that one smile, Lakhan could give away everything.

After the assembly ended... students were heading back to their classes...

Jiya walked straight up to Lakhan's bench, tapped his shoulder —

"The Shah Rukh Khan of Royal Glory... what a dialogue, bro!"

Lakhan, with a faint smile —

"When words come from the heart... they reach straight to another heart."

Jiya burst out laughing —

"And it definitely reached Kritika's heart, bro!"

Lakhan didn't say a word... he quietly opened his diary...

And wrote a new line...

"Today... when she smiled at me... the world just stopped."

Just then the classroom door opened... and Raju entered with full excited energy —

"Oye Lakhan bhai... Kritika should give you an award, bro! What dialogues you dropped!"

Jiya , in a chill mood, added —

"Yeah bro... but reality check — Lakhan still hasn't even talked to Kritika yet!"

Raju's reaction —

"Whaaaaat?! Then when are you gonna propose? After 12th?"

Lakhan, with calmness in his eyes, said —

"Love doesn't depend on time... it depends on the feeling..."

Both Raju and Jiya shouted together —

"Oyeeeeee Heroooooooo!"

But on the other side... on the corner bench...

Kritika was quietly looking in their direction...

And for the first time... she noticed Lakhan's smile...

And without even realizing... that smile found a little place in her heart...

Jiya , Raju, and Lakhan were chilling at their table...

But Lakhan's eyes... were stuck on Kritika and Riya's table...

Jiya , tease mode ON —

"Bro... don't stare too much... or you'll end up in a kidnapping case!"

Raju, full joke mode —

"At least go and say 'Hi' now..."

Lakhan, the true lover —

"Everything happens in its own time..."

Jiya , with a mischievous smile —

"But that time will only come... if you do something!"

Just then... Kritika got up to get her water bottle...

Her path passed right by Lakhan's table...

Heartbeat... slow motion...

She walked past...

And paused for a moment and said —

Kritika (softly):

"Nice lines today... that 'Thought of the Day' one..."

Lakhan literally froze... but replied in a calm voice —

"Thanks..."

Jiya and Raju looked at each other in total shock —

"Oooooo brooooo! Kritika just talked to you!!!"

Kritika smiled and walked ahead...

And another line got added to Lakhan's diary...

"For the first time... she took my name..."

Dreams began to sparkle in his eyes...

That moment... became the most precious page in his diary...

Jiya , in full emotional drama mode —

"Oye Raju... this moment should be written in history books!"

Raju, hyped up —

"Exactly... Lakhan didn't even talk or propose... still the girl spoke to him first! Bravo, Love Guru!"

Lakhan just smiled...And in his eyes, one line gleamed —

"For the first time... she took my name..."

Raju, full teasing mode —

"How much more time will you take, bro? Just go say — 'Kritika... I love you'..."

Jiya , taking it a notch higher —

"Yeah bro... what if tomorrow she's walking around with some other hero boyfriend?"

Lakhan, calmly —

"I don't rush... I wait for the right time..."

Meanwhile... from afar, even Kritika was sneaking glances at Lakhan...

Riya, tease mode ON —

"What are you looking at, Kritika? That's Lakhan... the silent killer..."

Kritika, with a soft smile —

"Maybe that's why... he feels so different..."

Riya —

"Seems like you're starting to like his dialogues a lot..."

Kritika, blushing —

"No... nothing like that... just really liked his 'Thought of the Day' line..."

Riya, with a naughty look —

"Hmm... just liked the line? Or his style too?"

Kritika, fully shy, went quiet...

And Lakhan... was writing in his diary...

"Love shouldn't be loud...It should be deep..."

Just then Jiya shouted —

"Oye Lakhan... the school trip is going to be announced tomorrow... and Kritika is coming too! Get ready, bro!"

A different kind of spark lit up Lakhan's face...

With a soft smile, he said —

"This isn't just a trip...It's a chance to change my destiny..."

"From tomorrow — a 2-day Educational Trip to Mountain Valley Resort..."

The whole school burst into excitement...

But for Lakhan...

This trip...was a signal to get closer to Kritika.

The morning breeze was fresh and cool.A gentle chill hung in the air, and outside the school's main gate — pure chaos and energy.

Sunglasses in one hand, group selfies being snapped, random dance moves, laughter, fun... it was the perfect start to an epic trip.

But in one quiet corner...stood Lakhan Agrawal.

Diary in hand... eyes searching for just one person.

Raju, buzzing with excitement, shouted —

"Bro Lakhan! This trip's gonna be explosive! Just watch!"

Jiya , never missing a chance to tease, added —

"The real explosion will be... if Kritika ends up on the seat next to you!"

Lakhan, with a soft grin —

"Seats aren't won by luck...They're earned by strategy."

And just as he said that... Kritika entered.

Simple jeans, a plain top, minimal makeup...but her natural beauty? It stood out effortlessly.

Laughing with her friends, she walked up to the school gate...and her presence brought a sparkle to Lakhan's eyes.

Jiya , with full-on drama, whistled —

"Oye look look... Queen Kritika has arrived!"

Raju, adding fuel to the fire —

"That's it bro... your heroine is officially here now!"

Lakhan... was quietly watching her every step.

With every laugh of hers... a silent smile formed on his lips.

Just then, the Trip In-Charge Teacher's voice echoed —

"All students, listen carefully! Bus No. 1 — Girls. Bus No. 2 — Boys!"

Disappointment level: 100.

Raju reacted instantly —

"What the hell man... boys and girls in different buses? What's even the point of this trip?"

Jiya , in classic chill mode —

"Relax bro... once we reach the resort, the game will be back on!"

Lakhan... quietly opened his diary again...

And wrote another line:

"Distance is necessary...The more the space, the deeper the connection becomes."

The bus had started moving.

Raju was in his full entertainment mode —Mimicry, singing old filmy songs, and his trademark over-the-top drama.

Lakhan sat by the window... diary in hand, eyes gazing out at the road, but mind lost somewhere else...

And then...one glance — from the Girls' Bus beside theirs.

Kritika was also sitting by the window...

As her eyes met Lakhan's...

A soft, quiet smile passed between them —A silent hello without a single word.

Raju, catching the moment, jumped in —

"Oye Lakhan! Dekh bro... full-on eye-lock going on!"

From the Girls' Bus, Jiya sent a message:

"Lakhanbro... first love exam begins! Ready ho?"

Lakhan's reply came back instantly:

"She's ready too...for the one who reads through her eyes..."

The boys' bus was full-on madness.Raju had turned his desk into a makeshift dholak — beating it like a pro, hyping everyone up.

But Lakhan...he was in a completely different zone.

He turned a page in his diary...and quietly wrote:

"The path from the eyes... leads straight to the heart."

Meanwhile, in the girls' bus...Kritika was chilling with her group — laughing at jokes, vibing to music...

But every now and then...her eyes drifted toward the boys' bus. Toward him.

Riya, in full teasing mode —

"Looks like Lakhan has made it to your daily 'watchlist' again, hmm?"

Kritika, with a soft smile —

"Woh... just like that... nothing special."

Riya, narrowing her eyes smartly —

"Hmmm... so you only like his 'Thought of the Day'?Or do you like how thoughtful he is?"

Kritika... totally in blush mode, went silent.Her smile said it all — even if her words didn't.

The bus stopped in front of the resort.

Green mountains in the distance, the soothing sound of waterfalls, and a cool breeze...

It felt straight out of a movie scene.

Jiya , bursting with energy, shouted —

"Oye Raju! This looks more like a honeymoon spot than a trip!"

Raju, turning to tease Lakhan, shot back —

"Bro... once the proposal is locked, the setting is locked too!"

The teachers began the room allotment...

Boys in one wing, girls in the other...

Jiya , leaning toward Lakhan, whispered into his ear —

"Lakhan... it's action time, bro. This trip could change everything for you..."

Lakhan closed his diary, a calm smile on his face, and said —

"The game... has just begun."

In the resort's garden area,students were chilling, playing games, snapping selfies...

But in one quiet corner...

Lakhan sat, eyes only on one face — Kritika.

And in his diary...he wrote a new page:

"The first gift of this morning was... her smile."

Lakhan thought to himself —

"This trip... will either become a memory... or a story..."

The cool breeze whispered secrets of the night...The sky above sparkled with stars, like dreams scattered in the dark.

At the center of the garden, a bonfire crackled softly —its glow lighting up faces filled with laughter, mischief, and the unspoken magic of the moment.

Then came Jiya , in her full drama mode, grabbing the mic like a host on a reality show —

"ALRIGHT PEOPLE... IT'S TRUTH & DARE TIME!!!"

The whole group roared —

"YEEEEEEEHHH!!!"

In the corner sat Lakhan, diary in hand, as always.But his heart — fixated on one presence only.

Kritika Patil.

Jiya spun the bottle dramatically...Time slowed. Heartbeats paused.

And the bottle stopped.

On Kritika.

Everyone exploded —

"Ooooooooo!!! Kritikaaaa!"

Jiya , with that mischievous glint in her eye —

"Your dare is... walk up to the most silent guy at this resort...and say one line to him."

No one needed a second to guess. All eyes turned to Lakhan.

Kritika hesitated for a moment...But then, with a soft smile, she stood up.

She took a breath.And started walking...One step. Two steps. Three steps...

With every step, Lakhan's heart pounded louder. But his face? Calm. Always calm.

She reached him.

Bonfire light danced on her face —painting her in golden warmth and quiet magic.

And then... she spoke. Softly. Sincerely.

"You don't speak much...But when you do...my heart listens."

For a second... the whole world froze.

No sound. No music. Just that one line...hanging between two hearts.

And then...

The group erupted! Clapping. Laughing. Hooting. Whistling.

Raju, losing his mind —

"Oyeeee HERO!!!! What a line brooooo!!!"
Jiya , clutching her heart —
"Heart se heart tak full Wi-Fi connected!"
And Lakhan?
No wild reaction. No dramatic reply.
Just one soft look into Kritika's eyes... A small, real smile.
And then, he opened his diary...and wrote:
"Tonight... for the first time...she came to me...without me ever calling her."

The night had its own kind of magic...And in the middle of that magic — two hearts, one path, and silence speaking everything.

Most students had returned to their rooms...But Kritika was still walking alone down the stone path in the resort garden. Her soft steps brushed against the grass like the cool breeze itself.

The moonlight peeked out from behind drifting clouds...And the cold wind played with her hair, as if even the night wanted to feel her presence.

Somewhere in the distance... a pair of eyes were fixed only on her —
Lakhan.
His diary was closed now...But his heart was still writing — just about her.
That's when Raju, in his usual filmy tone, came from behind —
"Bro... you gonna keep writing your diary, or finally live some real-life scenes too?"
Lakhan gave a calm smile... slipped the diary into his pocket,And without a word... started walking down the same path...
Slow steps... fast heartbeat.

Kritika felt the sound of his footsteps... turned gently to look...

And then —

Eyes met.

And for a second... time froze. No music. No noise. Just a still, quiet pause.

Lakhan (softly):

"Walking alone?"

Kritika, with a thoughtful smile —

"Sometimes... silence feels better..."

Lakhan:

"But sometimes... silence feels even more special when someone walks with you."

There was a pause.Not awkward. Not forced.

Just... beautiful.

They started walking, side by side.No plan. No direction.Just... together.

Every few seconds, their eyes would meet...And in that eye contact, the wind and the stars understood everything they didn't say.

A little later, Kritika asked —

"What do you write in that diary?"

Lakhan looked at her gently —

"Everything I can't say out loud..."

Kritika paused, looked at his face... and asked softly —

"Did you ever tell the person you write about?"

Lakhan met her eyes, calm but deep —

"Maybe... one day, she'll read it herself."

Kritika didn't say anything...

But her eyes held a quiet smile.The kind that didn't need words.

That night's walk...Wasn't a confession. Wasn't a proposal. But somehow... it was everything.

And just as they turned toward their separate rooms...

Lakhan took one last look at her, and thought:

"Tonight... even my loneliness felt complete."

Between the hills... a new morning bloomed.

There was a calmness in the air... as if the night had quietly etched something deep inside the heart.

Lakhan sat on the resort's terrace with his diary... sleep was less in his eyes, but the feelings were more.

Something was shifting inside him...

As if Kritika's one line had filled every page of his diary with a new emotion.

Raju walked in, stretching wide —

"Good morning, love guru! Get ready... The trekking trip's about to start!"

Jiya came in with a towel, teasing —

"Kritika all set too... and here you are, sitting with your diary? What's up... heart pressure rising?"

Lakhan, in a soft tone —

"She talked to me last night... and that's all I've been remembering."

Jiya , with wide eyes —

"Ooooo... the girl left, but the impact stayed!"

Group trekking had begun.

Boys, girls, teachers — everyone was walking in a single line. All around them: lush greenery, the sounds of birds, and the raw, untouched vibe of nature.

Kritika was walking slowly with a hiking stick... but every now and then, her eyes drifted toward Lakhan.

And Lakhan... quietly noticed every glance, every moment.

Then came a point where the path turned slippery.

Kritika's foot slipped. For a moment, she lost her balance...

And just then, a hand caught hers — tight, firm, protective.

Lakhan.

Lakhan (softly):

"Careful... these paths are beautiful, but unpredictable too..."

Kritika, eyes filled with quiet gratitude:

"Thank you..."

Lakhan, holding her gaze:

"Even if you had fallen, you'd have gotten back up...But I wouldn't have."

Kritika... stared at him for a moment...His face was serious, but his eyes carried a softness.From behind, Riya shouted:

"Oye Kritika! Holding hands with your hero now? What's going on?"

Everyone burst into laughter...

Lakhan gently let go of her hand...He didn't want to hold her because she had to — He wanted her to come closer... only if she wanted to.

The group sat down to rest near a small waterfall.

The sound of water crashing over the rocks created a natural calm, the kind that hugs your thoughts instead of interrupting them. Jiya and Raju were busy making reels, posing with exaggerated expressions and goofy dances.

Lakhan, as always, was quietly tucked in a corner — scribbling something into his diary, his world wrapped in words.

And then... she came.

Kritika.

She walked over slowly and sat beside him.

Her voice was soft — almost blending with the sound of water.

Kritika:

"I wanted to ask you something..."

Lakhan looked up, a little surprised —

"Ask."

Kritika:

"Why are you always so quiet? Why do you feel so... different from everyone else?"

Lakhan:

"Because when you're quiet... you can hear everything —The world...And you."

Kritika smiled gently —

"You listen to me?"

Lakhan, eyes tender:

"You don't hear yourself speak...But your silences? They say everything. And that's what I listen to."

She stared at him for a moment...Then, without saying anything, she gave the faintest blush and stood up — quietly walking away.

And Lakhan?

He opened his diary and wrote:

"She walked away...but for the first time, her silence said yes."

All the students were soaking in the mountain view — laughing, clicking selfies, playing with the breeze. But Lakhan stood alone at the edge of the cliffside garden... still, calm, lost in thoughts that had only one name.

Then, from behind, she came.

Kritika.

She walked up beside him, the soft sound of her steps blending with the rustling wind.

Kritika (softly):

"The view's beautiful, isn't it?"

Lakhan (without turning):

"Yeah...

But the most beautiful moment was...when you looked at me."

She smiled — gently, knowingly.

Kritika:

"You remember everything?"

Lakhan:

"How could I forget a moment...that began with you?"

There was silence again.

But this time... Kritika was the one to break it.

Kritika (in a slow whisper):

"You write about me... in that diary of yours, don't you?"

Lakhan froze — for a second. Shocked, exposed, yet strangely calm.

She smiled and continued —

Kritika:

"I can tell... I see it in your eyes."

Lakhan (heart speaking now):

"Then maybe one day...read it. When you're ready."

Kritika looked at him — not with surprise, not with hesitation... but something deeper.And then she said, barely above a whisper —

Kritika:

"Maybe...I already am."

And as the sun slowly dipped behind the mountains...

A new kind of light rose between them — Not loud, not fast...Just quietly real.

II

The Moment That Stayed...

The morning light had fully entered the resort now. Students were feeling a bit down — after all, two days of fun, bonding, and the soothing air of nature were about to be replaced by the rush of the city.

But for some people, this trip wasn't just a memory... it had become a turning point.

Lakhan stood with his bag in the lobby of the resort...For the first time, he zipped his diary closed.Some words were waiting in his heart with restlessness...But some things needed to be kept safe.The night he shared with Kritika... something he could never forget.

Jiya , in her usual teasing style, came over —

"What's up, Love Singh? Closed the diary? Is the story over?"

Lakhan, with a soft smile, replied —

"The story isn't over, Jiya ... I'm just waiting for a new page."

Raju, bursting into laughter —

"Bro, you're speaking like you're the writer of a Karan Johar movie!"

Jiya , placing her hand on Lakhan's shoulder, teased —

"Last night's walk with Kritika on the terrace... and today, silence? Did something happen?"

Lakhan, with a deep calm in his eyes, said —

"It didn't happen... but it did."

Jiya and Raju, both exchanged surprised looks...But then, they smiled, picked up their bags... and everyone's eyes were on their respective destinations.

As the bus started, Lakhan took one last glance at the resort...And in his heart, Kritika's smile... that silent connection...It had become permanent in his heart.

The bus had started moving.

The whole group was exhausted — some with earphones on, others in sleep mode...

But two people... whose hearts were still wide awake — Kritika and Lakhan.

Lakhan gazed out of the window, looking back at the hills they had just left behind...

And Kritika, sneakily, stole a glance at his reflection in the bus window...

Riya, with a teasing smile —

"What are you looking at, Kritika? The world's most calm lover?"

Kritika, softly —

"No... just... remembering his diary."

Riya, in shock —

"Just the diary? Or the words written inside it?"

Kritika fell silent for a moment...And then, slowly closed her eyes...

As if... the words from that night, the terrace walk, the conversations by the cliff... everything came rushing back to her.

Suddenly, the bus brakes squeaked, jerking slightly...Kritika's body shifted, and her hand slipped off the seat edge...But then, once again... a hand caught hers.

It was Lakhan's hand.

For a second, their hands were joined...And this time, Kritika didn't just let it be.. She held onto his hand, this time, with a soft sense of belonging.

In that one moment... love showed its claim.

Lakhan, softly —

"Do you keep falling... or have I just started catching you?"

Kritika, with a softness in her eyes —

"Maybe... it's both."

The rest of the bus was asleep...But there was a connection... quietly awakened in the silence between them.

The bus stopped at the school gate.Students grabbed their bags and started heading home.

Raju and Jiya were fully engaged in their chatter...

Lakhan picked up his bag, glanced at Kritika, and gave her a soft smile. And then, with a sense of certainty, he said:

"We'll meet again..."

Kritika, slowly, returned the same smile, her eyes reflecting a quiet promise:

"Definitely."

Lakhan placed the diary on the table, his mind wandering as he opened it and began writing:

"Sometimes, some people don't speak... they just hold your hand and say everything."

As he wrote, his phone buzzed, pulling him back to the present.

From: Kritika Patil

Message:

"Why do you look at me like that... as if there's a secret written in my eyes?"

Lakhan paused for a second, staring at the phone screen. A soft smile crept onto his face.

He quickly typed his reply:

"Because in your eyes... there really is a story written. Maybe one with my name in it."

Lakhan's phone buzzed again, interrupting the peaceful moment. He looked down at the screen, his eyes narrowing as he saw the message from an unknown number:

From Unknown Number:

"What's happening between you and Kritika... I'm watching everything. Be careful, Lakhan."

The calm smile that had lingered on Lakhan's face vanished instantly. His heart skipped a beat, and a cold shiver ran down his spine. Who could this be? How did they know about him and Kritika?

His fingers hovered over the screen for a moment. He knew something had shifted, but the question was: who was behind this warning, and what did they want?

He quickly glanced out the window, the surroundings feeling suddenly different, as if everything had changed with that one message.

New Twist Begins...

The tension in the air was thick now. The quiet moments between Lakhan and Kritika, once filled with warmth, now seemed to carry a shadow.

And so, the story wasn't just about love anymore... it was about uncovering the mysteries hidden beneath it all.

Lakhan still had the phone in his hand...

That message —

"I'm watching everything going on between you and Kritika. Be careful, Lakhan."

...was still glowing on the screen.

For the first time, his eyes didn't show fear... but deep thought.Who would have sent it? And why?

He picked up his diary... and wrote:

"When love arrives quietly...its enemies always make noise."

Just then, Jiya 's call came in.

Jiya (on the phone):

"Hey hero, stop sitting alone now... college starts tomorrow. You better be ready in your 'Royal Lover' uniform look!"

Lakhan (softly):

"Yeah... I'm ready... just lost in some thoughts."

Jiya :

"About that 'unknown' message?"

Lakhan, shocked —

"How do you know?"

Jiya :

"Kritika got something similar... She's a little shaken. And she's the one who told me."

A sharp concern flashed in Lakhan's eyes...

Lakhan:

"I'm calling her right now."

Kritika picked up the call — Her eyes held a hint of confusion, a trace of pain.

Lakhan (on the phone):

"Are you okay?"

Kritika:

"I don't know... someone sent me a message... the same line... that someone's watching us..."

Lakhan (in a calm voice):

"I'm here, aren't I? Nothing will happen. Maybe it's just a prank..."

Kritika, in a slightly emotional tone —

"But Lakhan... I'm starting to feel now... that what's happening between us... isn't just a phase from this trip."

Lakhan (softly):

"I knew from the beginning... this isn't just a moment... it's becoming a story."

Silence.

Then Kritika asked:

"What have you written about me in your diary?"

Lakhan, with a gentle laugh —

"From the first page to the last line... it's only you."

Kritika smiled...

And for the first time... without fear, she confessed her heart:

"I want to read every page of that diary..."

Lakhan's breath paused for a second...But he replied:

"Read it... when you're ready to be the heroine of that story..."

Lakhan stood near the college gate...Wearing his blue-white uniform, a leather bag slung over his shoulder, his diary tucked safely inside... and calmness in his eyes.

Jiya and Raju arrived —

"Oyeee bro!!! The whole college looks fresh today... and so do you."

Jiya leaned in and whispered —

"Kritika's here too... and the moment she saw you, she blushed... OMG!"

Lakhan looked into the distance...Kritika, dressed in a white kurta, was walking straight towards him — eyes full of confidence.

And just then...

An unknown guy... wearing a black hoodie... stepped in front of him.

Unknown Guy (to Lakhan):

"Your name's Lakhan, right? Think you're some kind of poet?"

Raju stepped in —

"Hey man, what's your problem?"

Hoodie Guy (with a cold smile):

"Just here to give a warning... Anyone who gets close to Kritika... never escapes the darkness that follows."

Jiya immediately stepped in front of Lakhan —

"Oye! What's your problem, huh?"

But the guy simply handed Lakhan a card...And walked away.

On the card, it said:

"I Know Your Story. But You Don't Know Mine Yet."

Jiya , Raju, Lakhan, and Kritika were all sitting together, deep in discussion.

Raju:

"Bro, this guy seriously sounds like some full-on psycho villain!"

Jiya :

"Kritika, is there something from your past? Any old story?"

Kritika, a little shocked —

"I knew a guy named Arjun... he used to wear the same kind of hoodie... but we blocked him a year ago."

Lakhan, with calm determination in his eyes, said —

"So the story started with Kritika... but now, I'll be the one to end it."

Kritika looked at him...And gently held his hand, softly saying:

"I'm with you..."

Lakhan opened his diary... and wrote:

"When someone's there to hold your hand...No matter how dark the road is they become your light."

That night, a note was left outside Lakhan's hostel room...

Note:

"Your diary... is no longer just yours."

Lakhan was shocked.

Lakhan stepped out of the hostel... calmness in his eyes, but a storm raging inside his mind.

Every single word from that note still echoed in his head —

"Your diary... is no longer just yours."

He told everything to Jiya ...

And now, Lakhan, Jiya , and Raju were sitting in a quiet corner of the college canteen — in full planning mode.

Jiya :

"Bro, someone got access to your diary... who could get that close?"

Raju:

"That guy... the one in the black hoodie. There was a possessiveness in his tone... like he's a file from Kritika's past trying to reopen himself."

Lakhan, gently running his fingers across the diary —

"For me, writing this diary was an art... but for someone else, it's turning into a weapon."

Jiya , with anger burning in her eyes —

"Whoever it is... they've crossed the line. You wrote this diary for that girl... and if someone tries to break it apart — we'll break them first."

Kritika was writing something on the board with chalk when a small note was tossed onto her desk.

The note read:

"Ever read a diary written in your name?"

"It's not just love... it's a painting of every moment of yours."

The chalk slipped from her hand and fell.

She immediately rushed out to the corridor, searching for Lakhan...

And when she finally found him, she asked —

"Did you write this?"

Lakhan looked straight into her eyes and simply said:

"No... but every word felt like it came from my heart."

Something shifted inside Kritika...She couldn't understand who to trust anymore.

Lakhan (softly):

"I feel like someone's trying to break the truth between us... Kritika, is there something you want to tell me?"

Kritika, a bit confused, replied —

"There was someone... who came into my life once. Arjun. He was friendly at first, but then turned possessive... I blocked him eventually..."

Lakhan (serious):

"It could be him."

Kritika, in a faint voice —

"He even stole my diary once... during the college fest..."

A mix of anger and pain flared in Lakhan's eyes.

"Kritika, no matter what happens now... I'm with you. But if he does anything again... I won't let him go unpunished."

Lakhan was pulling his diary out of his bag when a voice came from behind:

"Love doesn't happen by writing it... it happens by having it."

It was him — the guy in the black hoodie.

Arjun.

Lakhan (firmly):

"You're just the wrong page from Kritika's past. There's no chapter left for you in this story."

Arjun:

"But every story has a villain, Lakhan. And between you two... I am that villain."

Lakhan (with an intense gaze):

"You're not even worthy of being a villain...You're just a leftover pain... who still hasn't learned from time."

Arjun held up a copy of the diary —

"Yes... this is a copy of the story you wrote...One that's no longer just yours now, it's mine too."

Lakhan snatched the diary out of his hands...

Arjun (with a warning):

"Your time together... is about to flip."

Kritika was staring at a blank page in the diary...And inside, a voice kept echoing

"I need to tell him... everything. Everything."

She picked up her phone, and sent a message to Lakhan:

"I want to meet you... tonight... on the terrace."

Lakhan saw Kritika's message...

But just then, a small note slipped under his room door.

It read:

"Kritika isn't safe with you...If you tell her the truth... you'll lose her."

Lakhan picked up his diary...

And said quietly to himself:

"Then so be it...Let it be the truth — But I won't stay silent anymore."

Kritika had reached the terrace...

At that moment, everything inside her was calm... but a volcanic emotion was rising within.Under the moonlit night... wearing her white kurta, she had come to find answers to the questions of her heart.

Lakhan also arrived — holding the diary, his eyes filled with truth...

They stood facing each other...Between them, only a breeze swirled, intensifying the beat of their hearts.

Kritika (breaking the silence):

"What's happening, Lakhan...? I'm scared..."

Lakhan (softly):

"I'm scared too, Kritika...But this time... I don't want to run away."

Kritika, her eyes filling with tears, spoke:

"That note... Arjun... his presence... my diary... your diary... everything... my past is pulling me back!"

Lakhan, looking straight into her eyes, said:

"Your past was just one page...I want you to become the entire book of my life..."

Kritika wiped her tears with her hand, and said:

"Do you know when I realized I had become a part of you?"

Lakhan (with a soft smile):

"Don't tell me... just let me feel it..."

Kritika:

"When you held me at the edge of the cliff...That touch... those eyes.. It was the first time I felt...That I could see my place in someone's eyes..."

Lakhan opened the diary...And read aloud an old line:

"With you... I could finally hear my own voice."

Tears streamed down Kritika's face...

And slowly, she walked up to Lakhan... and held his hand...

Kritika (whispering):

"I'm ready... to read that diary..."

Lakhan, with love in his eyes —

"Then read it... when you're ready to write your name in that story too..."

Kritika (smiling through her tears):

"Then write it... from today, let my name be on every page."

In the distant darkness...A shadow stood in the corner of the terrace, watching everything unfold.

Arjun.

In his hand, he held a photo of Lakhan's diary...And he typed something on his phone:

"Now, I'll play this game in the name of love...Now, I am the writer of this story."

Arjun:

"To separate you two, I don't need words anymore...I just need moments to change everything."

Lakhan walked into the campus calmly...But there was something different in his eyes today — a quiet peace, a final decision.

Jiya and Raju came rushing toward him:

Jiya :

"Bro! Did you see what Arjun did?!"

Raju:

"He posted a page from your diary on his story... the one with Kritika's name in it! It's gone viral, bro!"

Lakhan, gently holding his diary —

"What was written with love...has now been turned into something cheap in people's eyes."

Jiya (furious):

"This is too much! That guy's crossed the line now!"

Lakhan (calm but confident):

"He's said everything he wanted to say...Now it's my turn."

The principal had summoned all students after the social media scandal.

Lakhan stepped up on stage —Diary in hand... standing in front of the entire college.

Lakhan (in a firm tone):

"I'm Lakhan Agrawal...And today, I opened this diary in front of you all...Because this is the truth of my heart... which someone turned into drama."

The entire hall went silent.

Lakhan:

"There's nothing wrong in writing about love...But stealing someone's written love... only a coward does that."

Phones started buzzing in the audience...

At the back of the crowd, Arjun stood — burning with rage. But now... everyone was looking at him — The villain had been unmasked.

Just then, the auditorium doors opened...

Kritika walked in —

Dressed in white, grace in every step.Every eye turned toward her.

She walked straight to the stage... stood beside Lakhan...Took the mic, and said:

Kritika (clear and proud):

"I'm Kritika Patil...And yes — I'm the girl this diary was written for."

The crowd gasped.

Kritika:

"What was written... was love — not shame.And the one who tried to make it look cheap... only exposed his own character."

The audience erupted in applause.

Kritika gently took Lakhan's hand — right in front of everyone.

Kritika:

"I haven't read the diary...But I've read the boy... who respected me in every page he ever wrote."

Jiya and Raju hugged Lakhan...

Raju (teary-eyed):

"Bro... you didn't just get a girlfriend, you got god-level respect too!"

Jiya :

"This turned into a full-blown movie!"

Lakhan sat on a bench with Kritika...

Kritika:

"Were you ever scared?"

Lakhan (with calm eyes):

"No... because I always knew...Love doesn't need proof, just presence."

Kritika smiled.

And in that diary, a new page was written:

"When the world exposes every secret...sometimes just holding one hand is enough to hold everything together."

On the outer wall of the college, under the dim evening lights...a line stood out in bold red spray paint:

"To Be Continued...Arjun is not done yet."

III

When Love Went Public for the First Time

The college garden was calm.Students walked by, some throwing curious glances, others stealing smiles.But on that one bench, time had slowed down.Lakhan and Kritika sat together — quietly, hands held.Not hiding. Not afraid.Just... there. At the moment.

Kritika (softly):

"Something feels different... sitting with you like this."

Lakhan (closing his diary, smiling):

"Until now, I was writing about you.From today, I want to live with you."

A gentle breeze passed.

From a little distance, Jiya and Raju peeked from behind a tree.

Jiya (whispering, playful):

"The heroine said yes... there's no climax left now!"

Raju (mock serious):

"Arey pagli, climax toh abhi aana baaki hai…The villain hasn't made his final move yet."

Behind them, unnoticed —

A phone camera zooms in on Lakhan and Kritika.A click. A shadow. A message being typed.

And somewhere, not far…

Arjun watches the screen.

Smirking.

Calculating.

It started with a single ping. Then, like wildfire — the "CONFESSION FAKE OR FACT?" The post exploded across the college network.

A blog, posted anonymously.

Kritika's name. Diary excerpts — but twisted.

Lines that were never written.Emotions turned into mockery.Love, painted as lust. Poetry turned into poison.

Kritika had picked up the phone — clinging to one last hope. But what she got… was another scar.

Text from Unknown Number:

"Now everyone will read… where you were only mine."

In that moment, it was like her breath froze.For the first time, her pain turned into rage.

Kritika (shouting):

"Enough! I'm not a chapter in anyone's twisted story!"

She threw the phone — it hit the wall, the screen shattered. But her strength didn't.Riya ran to her, hand on her shoulder, eyes full of worry.

Riya (concerned):

"What happened, Kritika?!"

Kritika (tears in her eyes, voice burning):

"Arjun… he hasn't just invaded my privacy…He's made my self-respect go viral. He's no longer just a past lover —

he's a public predator."

Riya (firmly):

"You have Lakhan on your side... tell him everything. Don't fight this alone."

Jiya and Raju came running down the corridor, breathless, straight to Lakhan.

Jiya (panting):

"Bro... fake pages from your diary went viral under Kritika's name!"

Raju:

"The girls' group is shocked... boys' chats are full of memes now..."

Lakhan's expression turned still, serious.He pulled out his phone immediately and dialed Kritika.

Ringtone......then her voice — fragile, trembling.

Lakhan (softly):

"Are you okay?"

Kritika (in a breaking voice):

"No, Lakhan... I was writing my own diary... someone turned it into a circus. Twisted my love, my emotions... my respect."

Lakhan (calm but strong):

"Whoever did this... doesn't matter. Because now, you're not just my responsibility...You are my respect."

On the other end, a shaky breath.

Kritika (almost crying):

"I feel broken, Lakhan... people are judging me for words I never wrote."

Lakhan (with firm resolve):

"Then let's go... let's stand in front of them and put ourselves back together. Where they read the fake... we'll speak the truth."

A moment of silence...

And then a faint, tearful smile on Kritika's lips.

Kritika (soft whisper):

"I'm with you, Lakhan... even in front of the whole world now."

Lakhan and Kritika entered the auditorium.

A heavy silence swept the hall — every eye on them.

Lakhan calmly stepped onto a table, took the mic into his hand.

Lakhan (to the crowd, voice steady but fierce):

"I'm a writer...But I'm not a coward. The one who violated the words of a diary —his truth will also be exposed... publicly."

Gasps filled the room. Whispers broke the silence.

He continued, eyes scanning the crowd.

Lakhan:

"Whoever created that blog —didn't just attack Kritika's character...They tried to stain her dignity.And now...they won't just face me —they'll face the law."

The crowd fell silent again — not from fear, but respect.Because in that moment, it wasn't just about love. It was about standing for what was right

The officer looked up from the screen, voice firm:

Cyber Cell:

"ID tracked.

Name: Arjun Suryavanshi."

Lakhan stood still for a moment... then took a deep breath.

He whispered, more to his soul than to the world:

Lakhan (under his breath):

"You kept stealing words...Now I'll erase your name."

His eyes didn't show rage. They showed purpose.

The officer slid a file across the table toward Lakhan. The fluorescent light above flickered slightly, matching the tension in the room.

Officer (firm tone):

"Yeh hai us IP address ka trace.

Blog creator: Arjun Suryavanshi.

Tumhare college ka former student. Last year suspension ke baad disappear ho gaya tha."

Lakhan slowly opened the file, glanced at the name, then closed it just as calmly. His voice had no anger — just icy focus.

Lakhan (cold tone):

"Ab wapas aaya hai... meri kahani todne."

Officer:

"Hum legal action le rahe hain.Par tum dono ko media se bachke rehna hoga — ye case public ho gaya toh backlash ho sakta hai."

Lakhan stood up, file in hand. His eyes no longer showed fear, or even pain — just unshaken resolve.

Lakhan (under his breath):

"Ab wo meri diary nahi... mera jawab padega."

Kritika sat curled in the corner of her room. Phone turned off, lights barely glowing — the shadows seemed to echo her guilt. Her eyes were tired, not from lack of sleep, but from carrying the weight of judgment.

Riya slowly walked in and sat beside her, concern laced in every word.

Riya (softly):

"You were strong, Kritika... what happened to that fire?"

Kritika (voice breaking):

"I was strong... until people started talking about my diary. Now every eye reads me... judges me... like I'm just a book written for scandal."

Riya gently held her hand.

Riya:

"But that book was written for you, not against you. And no one gets to rewrite it without your permission."

Tears finally rolled down Kritika's cheeks — silent, painful, heavy.

Just then, Lakhan entered — no drama, no noise. He quietly sat in front of her, eyes filled with unwavering calm.

Lakhan:

"I'm not here to count your tears, Kritika...I'm here to steal them away, so you can find your smile again."

Kritika (sobbing):

"I don't even know what's true anymore...Every line, every word... feels like a trial I never agreed to."

Lakhan:

"Trials are meant to prove the truth...And you are the truth, Kritika."

He took out his diary... carefully opened it... and placed one worn page in front of her.

Lakhan:

"This... was the first page I ever wrote for you. When all you were to me... was a smile. Just one smile."

Kritika (shaken):

"But Arjun turned that smile into a weapon..."

Lakhan (gently, but firmly):

"Then let me be the soldier who shields you from that weapon."

He reached for her hand — not to save her, but to stand beside her.

Arjun sat hunched over his laptop, eyes sharp, movements precise. On his screen — a video editing software open, timelines stacked with layers of sound and visuals.

He dragged a voice note — a real one from Kritika, soft and emotional.

Then, with cold precision, he overlaid one of Lakhan's most heartfelt diary quotes — twisted just enough to change the context.

Arjun (smirking):

"Let's make love look like manipulation."

He added a dramatic filter, slowed down Kritika voice for effect, and threw in subtle background music that made it feel like a confession.

Finally, in bold letters, he typed the title:

"TRUTH REVEALED: THE GIRL BEHIND THE LINES"

He previewed it once — eyes scanning every second like a predator setting a trap.

Arjun (to himself, dark tone):

"This video... will flip the whole damn story. And Lakhan, while you keep writing... I'll rewrite everything."

His finger hovered over the button.

"SCHEDULE POST — Tomorrow, 6 PM."

He clicked.

Arjun (leaning back, eyes glinting):

"Tick-tock, Lakhan. Tomorrow... your fairytale dies."

— Screen fades to black. Countdown begins.

Students stood frozen mid-step, their eyes darting toward Kritika and Lakhan. Murmurs swirled in the air — hushed voices, darting glances, quiet judgments.

Some smirked.

Some judged.

Some... just stared.

But Kritika didn't lower her gaze.

Instead, she turned toward Lakhan — and in one bold move, tightly held his hand.

A loud gasp escaped the crowd. Whispers paused mid-air.

Kritika (firm, loud enough for all):

"Mujhe farak padta hai…Par sirf us insaan ke liye jo mere har farak mein saath chalta hai."

Her words echoed — strong, fearless, beautiful.

For a moment, silence hung like truth in the sky.

Then—

Jiya and Raju — standing near the café steps, their eyes watery — started clapping.

Jiya (wiping a tear, smiling):

"Queen energy activated."

Raju (sniffling, laughing):

"Bhai ki heroine ne pura scene loot liya."

And just like that…Judgments turned into respect. Whispers turned into admiration.

Kritika and Lakhan — still hand in hand — stood not as a couple fighting rumors, but as a team rewriting their own story.

"Time reveals everything…But when love stands tall in front of the world…Even the loudest lies fall silent."

The Principal stood on stage…All the students were seated, and the entire campus buzzed with just one topic — Lakhan & Kritika viral video.

A projector screen was ready behind him.

The Principal spoke:

"Someone auto-scheduled a video on the campus server. We're going to play it openly, so everyone can understand the truth."

Lakhan and Kritika sat together, holding each other's hand tightly.Lakhan had kept the diary closed — today, it wasn't about writing love…It was about proving it.

The room was silent. The screen flickered.The play button was pressed.

And now, only one question echoed in everyone's mind —

"What's the truth?"

The screen lit up with a black background.
Kritika's name flashed in bold.

And then the audio began — Kritika's edited voice played. Emotional quotes from the diary were cut, rearranged, and twisted...changing their entire meaning.

The crowd was stunned. Some students laughed. Some whispered in disbelief. A few just stared, speechless.

Raju (furious):

"This is pure editing, bro! Full-on manipulation!"

Jiya (clenching her fists):

"Arjun's crossed every line now... this isn't just drama — it's full-on character assassination!"

Tears streamed down Kritika's face...

She got up and began to run out of the auditorium —
But Lakhan grabbed her hand.

Lakhan:

"No, Kritika... the time to run is over."

He walked with her — straight to the stage, in front of the entire auditorium.

Lakhan (taking the mic):

"You all watched an edited video and chose to doubt the truth? I'm the writer of that diary. And if someone wants to turn my words into a weapon...Then fine — today, I'll open that diary... right here, in front of all of you!"

The crowd was stunned.

He took out the diary...And started reading the real pages — Where Kritika's smile, her pain, her dreams — lived in every word.

Lakhan (reading aloud):

"The smile on her face... is the first sunrise of my day.And if anyone tries to steal that smile...Just know — they've never truly loved anyone in their life."

Girls' Group (whispering):

"Is this... the real diary?"

Boys' Group (in awe):

"Bro... this is what true love looks like."

Raju and Jiya moved through the students, speaking loudly:

Raju:

"You all shared Arjun's video, didn't you?"

Jiya :

"Then now share this diary too... let the real version go viral!"

Arjun was staring at his laptop screen, eyes wide, fists clenched.

On the trending list, the hashtag #DiaryWithYourName — ORIGINAL had climbed to the top.

Arjun (gritting his teeth):

"I tried to write a story against a writer? This isn't just a mistake... this is my downfall."

Just then, his phone vibrated. A new message flashed on the screen:

"We know where you are. Cops incoming."

Arjun's face turned pale.

Panic replaced the arrogance in his eyes. The hunter... was now the hunted.

Kritika, with tears in her eyes, rests her head gently on Lakhan's shoulder. The noise of the world fades away — it's just the two of them now, in a silence that says more than words ever could.

Kritika (whispering):

"You became my voice, Lakhan... and gave me back the strength I lost."

Lakhan (softly, with a slight smile):

"I'm not your hero, Kritika...I'm just a human...who's ready to fight every word that ever tried to break you."

Their bond wasn't built on grand gestures —It was stitched together by trust, pain, and words that mattered. And now, every eye that once judged... now watched in silence — as real love healed in public.

"When lies go viral...The voice of truth rises from pain. And in that voice... a person becomes more than a memory — They become just one name — Your Name."

Kritika was sitting quietly in the corner of the library, eyes heavy with fatigue, mind clouded with thoughts.

Suddenly, the college clerk walked in holding an envelope.

Clerk:

"Kritika Patil? This is a legal notice for you."

Students nearby turned their heads in shock, some whispering, others just staring.

With trembling hands, Kritika opened the envelope.

Notice:

"Defamation & Emotional Harassment Case Filed By: Arjun Suryavanshi"

It also mentioned "unlawful public shaming and privacy breach."

Her face turned pale.

Jiya and Raju rushed to her.

Jiya (panicked):

"Bro! Kritika got a legal notice... Arjun has filed a case against her!"

Lakhan (cold whisper):

"Everyone leave... I need to meet her now."

Kritika, with tears in her eyes, stood in front of Lakhan.

Kritika:

"I thought everything was clear... but Arjun... now he's infiltrated even my legal system."

Lakhan (calm voice):

"He's just a name, Kritika... the real warrior is you."

Kritika:

"I'm not strong, Lakhan... I feel like I've lost."

Lakhan takes her hand firmly.

Lakhan:

"You haven't lost... you're just tired. And as long as I'm here... even if you fall, I'll catch you."

Arjun was on the phone with his lawyer.

Arjun:

"I had to drag her to the courtroom. That's when the diary will be burned... and then Lakhan will see me as a villain, not just a writer."

As he spoke, his gaze landed on a folder labeled: "Kritika_2019_Video".

Curious, he opened the file.

It was an old video of Kritika, in a vulnerable moment from her past — something never meant to go public.

He smirks, a dangerous plan forming in his mind.

Lakhan filed the complaint again — this time with a hard drive in hand, handing it over to the police.

Cyber Officer:

"This is clear. Arjun hacked into Kritika's gallery and stole her private data. It's a punishable offense."

Lakhan (firmly):

"I don't want this to be just a case... I want it to be an example."

Lakhan stands in front of all the students, his voice strong, clear, and determined.

Lakhan:

"I wrote a diary for Kritika...But now, I'm writing a new story for her — Where every girl fights for her own dignity."

The crowd begins to applaud, slowly at first, but gaining momentum as his words sink in.

Then, Kritika steps onto the stage. With grace and confidence, she takes the microphone.

Kritika:

"I am Kritika. I'm not the muse of a writer... I am the writer of my own story."

She takes a matchstick from her pocket, her fingers steady, and pulls out a printed copy of Arjun's fake blog post. The room falls silent as she holds it up.

Then, without hesitation, she sets it on fire, letting it burn in front of everyone — symbolizing the destruction of lies.

Kritika (holding the burnt paper in her hand, voice strong and resolute):

"You used to protect your diary...But when the world turns that diary into a weapon...It should be in the hands of a fighter, not just a writer."

Principal Sir stands on the stage, speaking into the mic with a serious tone:

"Today, we will hold a special session — 'Freedom of Expression vs Digital Attack'. And on the panel will be: Kritika Patil, Lakhan Agrawal, and... Arjun Suryavanshi."

The entire college gasps in shock.

Jiya (whispers to Raju):

"Bro! Arjun's gonna be on stage? With them, face to face?"

Raju (wide-eyed):

"This just turned into a real-life courtroom drama... but on campus."

Lakhan gently holds Kritika's hand —

Lakhan:

"Are you okay?"

Kritika (with a steady voice):

"Until now, everyone only heard my voice...Today, I want to see the truth in their eyes."

Lakhan (softly):

"When you speak... every word will feel like a page from the diary."

Arjun takes the mic first.

Arjun (with a fake calm tone):

"I just want to say one thing...If someone writes personal feelings in a diary, and those words go public...then should we blame the writer — or the audience?"

The crowd falls silent.

Then Kritika stands up.

Kritika:

"Arjun, you didn't just steal a diary...You shattered the boundaries of dignity."

Arjun:

"You have no proof."

Kritika:

"Proof isn't always needed...When a girl's every tear holds truth, she doesn't need evidence to be believed."

The crowd bursts into applause.

Lakhan steps forward and takes the mic.

Lakhan:

"I wrote that diary for you, Kritika...But Arjun turned it into a battlefield. Today, I'm not just a writer...I'm a witness."

The Principal calls Arjun to the center.

Principal (firmly):

"We've reviewed the cyber evidence against you.You were suspended before... but returning just to disgrace this institution?"

A pause. Then he pulls out an official document.

"You are hereby expelled... and reported to the cyber crime authorities."

Gasps echo through the auditorium. Arjun stands frozen. The weight of consequences is finally catching up.

Lakhan and Kritika were sitting quietly on the bench.The chaos of the day had settled, but their hearts were still carrying the aftershock — softer now, like rain after a storm.

Kritika (gazing at the sky):
"You know... when I burned that diary, it felt like I was destroying my past."

Lakhan (gently):
"You didn't burn the diary...you just let the truth shine through the fire of all the lies."

She looked at him — tears not of sadness, but release.
Kritika:
"So... what do we do now?"

Lakhan (with a soft smile):
"Now... we start writing new pages.Where love isn't just words... it becomes a voice."

They sat in silence, a beautiful silence — the kind that doesn't need filling. Just two people... rewriting their story, one truth at a time.

"Diary With Your Name is no longer just a secret of one girl —it has become a voice, an answer for an entire society."

IV
When the First Bond of Love Was Born from Words...

The morning sun shimmered gently...But today, the diary was red — Because Lakhan was ready to begin a new chapter.

From a distance, Jiya and Raju watched, their faces lit with excitement.

Jiya (grinning):

"Is he going to propose?"

Raju (teasing):

"Bro's already fought on stage... now it's time to win in love!"

Dressed in a white and peach kurti, Kritika walked up to Lakhan with a soft smile.

Kritika:

"Why is this diary... red?"

Lakhan (gently):

"Because now, every page will be written in love."

He opened the diary... and read the first page:

"I'm a writer...I feel every word...And when I begin to write about love, Only one name escapes my heart — yours."

Kritika kept looking at him — eyes holding a perfect blend of tears and a smile.

Lakhan handed her the diary:

Lakhan:

"This is a relationship I'm offering...Not a contract, not a demand...Just the first page of love. If you want... you can write the rest."

Kritika held the diary close to her heart.

Kritika:

"I'll write... every page... but on one condition."

Lakhan:

"What is it?"

Kritika (smiling):

"I want to write your every mood, every thought, every fight, every peace... Because you're the writer...But I'm the heroine of your story too."

Her mom and dad were sitting at the dining table when Kritika quietly walked in, her eyes filled with clarity and calm.

Dad (firmly):

"We found out everything. The video... the diary... all of it. The college has filed a complaint too."

Mom (concerned):

"Kritika, what was all this?"

Kritika (with quiet confidence):

"All of that... was a lie. And the one I stand with — Lakhan — he only writes the truth. He doesn't know how to lie."

Dad (sternly):

"Was it really necessary to write a love story on the first page of your career?"

Kritika:

"Love isn't just a story... it's strength. And Lakhan is my strength."

Mom:

"Do you really trust this boy?"

Kritika:

"I don't just trust him...I trust every word he's ever written."

Lakhan sat alone in his room, writing in his diary...

Diary Line:

"When a girl doesn't just believe in your love...but in the words you've written...that's when you know — you're not just a writer anymore...you've become her truth."

Kritika's mom and dad sat across from her, the room heavy with silence. Her dad's voice finally broke through — firm, composed, but serious.

Dad (in a serious tone):

"I have no problem with Lakhan as a person...But I can't let your future hang in the balance."

Kritika (softly but steadily):

"I understand, Papa... but every step I've taken with him... has been with complete awareness."

Mom (calm but concerned):

"If you both are serious about this...Then prove it — with responsibility. Your MBA entrance exams are around the corner...And if Lakhan truly wants a future with you...

He should focus on building a career, not chasing controversy."

Kritika looked down, taking in their words — then looked back up and gently nodded.

Kritika:

"...Theek hai, Papa." ("Okay, Papa.")

Lakhan was on a call, the voice of the poetry club in-charge buzzing with excitement on the speaker.

In-Charge (on call):

"Lakhan... we had submitted some of your poems for a national level competition a while back..."

Lakhan (surprised):

"I didn't even know about that..."

In-Charge:

"You've been shortlisted — Lucknow Literature Fest. It's a big platform, Lakhan. You'll be able to present your words in front of the whole country."

A wave of mixed emotions passed across Lakhan's face — joy tangled with hesitation.

Lakhan:

"Let me... think about it."

He hangs up the phone... but his mind drifts back to Kritika's words:

"If Lakhan really wants something... he needs to build a career, not chase controversy..."

He walks toward the window, silently staring at the sky — For the first time, his story had reached a crossroad...Where both love and dreams were asking him to choose.

The breeze was gentle, but the silence between them was heavier than ever.

Kritika:

"My dad... wants me to put my career first before anything else."

Lakhan (softly):

"He's not wrong...I've always lived inside words, Kritika — But now it's time to win in real life too."

Kritika:

"I'm scared, Lakhan...Can we really handle all of this together?"

Lakhan:

"If you're ready... I'll walk every step with you. But if you hesitate... I'll take a step back."

Kritika (shocked):

"Why?"

Lakhan (eyes slightly wet, voice steady):

"Because I can't let you break — Not in love... and definitely not in your dreams."

A soft pause followed, where hearts spoke louder than words. And maybe, just maybe... This silence was a promise too.

Lakhan sits alone, staring at his diary — but tonight, he doesn't write.

Lakhan (voiceover):

"For the first time... I had to stay away from my diary. But if this distance... becomes the path that leads me closer to her, Then I'll keep writing her name in every waiting word."

He slowly closes the diary, places it aside, and opens his laptop.

The screen lights up — Lucknow Poetry Fest: Registration Form.

Lakhan (softly, to himself):

"I always wanted to be a writer...Now it's time to win the world — one word at a time."

Lakhan stood still — ticket in hand, but eyes locked on Kritika's name flashing on his phone screen. A moment of silence, a storm within.

Raju (anxiously):

"Bro... just send her one message. You never know when you'll get to talk to her again."

Lakhan (with quiet pain):

"No, Raju...When I return with victory...I don't want to bring just results — I want to bring respect."

Jiya gently touches his shoulder, her voice calm but firm.

Jiya :

"We'll be cheering for you every step of the way... online and from the heart. Just don't lose faith in yourself."

The train horn blares in the background — a sharp call of destiny.

Lakhan exhales slowly, puts the phone back into his pocket...

And steps onto the train.

The journey begins — not just to Lucknow, but toward proving his voice, his worth, and the truth of his love.

Books lay open... equations half-solved... pens moving, but the mind elsewhere.

Kritika stares blankly at a physics formula, but her heart was somewhere in Lucknow — walking beside a boy with a red diary.

Riya (walking in, arms folded):

"You're sitting in the study zone...But your mind? Lost far, far away."

Kritika's voice quivers, her eyes glancing toward the window like she's searching for him in the wind.

Kritika (softly):

"I want to talk to Lakhan... I really do. But something holds me back...I feel like if I call him... I might break his focus."

Riya (sitting beside her):

"You know what's crazy?You think love is a distraction...But he thinks of you as his direction."

The crowd is massive. Camera flashes flicker. Spotlight on the stage. And then, enters — Lakhan Agrawal.

He walks slowly to the mic, red diary in hand, calm but intense. He flips it open and reads aloud... his voice low, poetic, personal.

Lakhan (reading):

"I write... because it's the only way I can talk to you. I pause... so that maybe, you'll linger a little longer in my words. I live... in the hope that one day,you'll read the line hidden between my verses... the one that only says — you."

The hall holds its breath. Silent. Still.

Then — a single clap.

Another.

And then the room erupts — standing ovation, teary smiles, hands clapping with heart.

The phone screen glows faintly in the dark. Kritika sits on her bed, phone in hand, eyes wet with tears. Her thumb hovers over the "send" button, the text typed but never sent.

Text on screen:

"I need to talk to you... When you come back..."

Her heart races, torn between the words she wants to say and the silence she's forced to keep.

She breathes in deeply, her gaze drifting to the ceiling, lost in her thoughts. Her mind wanders back to Lakhan, to the words he just shared with the world... and to the promise she had made to herself.

The sound of the message notification from her phone breaks the stillness.

Riya's text on the screen pops up:

Riya (text):

"If your heart says it, then send it. You both are meant for each other."

Kritika glances at the phone, her fingers shaking slightly. She looks at the text again... and slowly, with a quiet resolve, she presses "Send".

The message is sent. A single tear falls down her cheek, but this time, it's not without doubt. It's from hope.

"I won...But the biggest reward —was just a phone call that still hasn't come."

The entire campus was decorated.

Banners read:

"Welcome Back, Our Writer Star – Lakhan Agrawal"

Lakhan steps down from the bus... holding a gold medal from the literature fest and a laminated certificate in hand.

Jiya and Raju are the first to hug him.

Jiya :

"You've brought such honor to the entire college, bro!"

Raju:

"You were always a poet... but now you've become a public figure!"

All the students are lined up, asking for autographs.

But Lakhan... his eyes are searching for just one face — Kritika.

Kritika was staring intently at a page in her diary...

She picked up her phone ten times, and put it down ten times.

Riya:

"You're not going to meet him?"

Kritika:

"He's won now... he doesn't need me anymore."

Riya:

"In love, it's not about need, it's about habit...And you are his deepest habit."

Kritika opened her diary... and wrote just three words:

"Come back home."

V

when emotions surface

The cold morning breeze was roaming in every corner of the campus, but there was a strange warmth in Lakhan's heart - that confused warmth which is felt only when everything seems fine, but the heart is saying... something is wrong. Kritika was looking a little dierent that day. There was the same smile on her face, but something else was written in her eyes. She was talking normally, but every answer seemed rehearsed. As if she was trying to hide something. Jiya noticed - "Oye Lakhan, why is Kritika silent today? Usually you are silent." Lakhan just gave a slight smile, "Maybe you are tired..." But there was a strange feeling in his heart. Every time Kritika looked at him, there was something in her eyes - neither love, nor anger... just a strange silence.when emotions surface.

Raju came with full energy, "Oye bhai! Today posters are going to be put up in the campus! The Dean said there is some special announcement!" Lakhan just smiled a little.

He was about to say something when suddenly a crowd of students gathered at one place. Everyone was looking at the same poster. Lakhan and Raju also ran. It was written on the poster - "Someone had written it for a name... but now that name is in front of everyone." Below it was written - **"From the Diary of Lakhan Agrawal - Written for Kritika Patil"** And below it was written that line... a line which was only on page no. 17 of Lakhan's diary. Lakhan's face lost its colour for the first time. Jiya says, "Bhai, you never told this line to anyone, right?" Lakhan's voice became cold, "No... this was only in my diary." Kritika came, stopped in front of the poster, saw that line... and said only this much - "I did not write this." Lakhan looked into her eyes - but that day, he did not hear the voice of his heart.

Voices started coming from nearby - "This was a love story of both of you, right?" "Don't do drama friend, Kritika must have leaked it..." "This is a publicity stunt..." Lakhan was silent. Kritika too. And between the two – a line from a diary... a rift was created between two hearts. But who knew – this was just the beginning. What was left... only Raj was left to be written in it. There was pain hidden in Lakhan's eyes, but he thought it was better to keep quiet. Kritika's smile was still the same, but there was a deep darkness in her eyes. Both of them were silent, but the silence between them created a noise. Jiya secretly held Lakhan's hand - "Bro, everything will be fine..." But Lakhan knew, now everything had changed. And then... one more thing, one more secret, was about to come their way. Chapter will continue soon.......in PART 2

Final Note By The Author

I never thought that the words I had written only for myself, will be read by the world one day. "Diary With Your Name" is not just a story – it is a part of my heart. If you have ever missed someone without saying anything, just wanted them from the heart...Then this diary is somewhere yours too. It is possible that every page is filled with his memories... whom you could never forget. Thank you for feeling that pain... which I had only written, you lived it.

"Some love... is just for writing. And some names... are never for calling, just for living."

– Lakhan Agrawal

SOME LINES NEVER FADE...

- I kept writing, she kept reading...
- Her one smile was my every victory.
- I wrote every moment in the name of the one I couldn't get.
- She never became mine... but I lived in her every time
- Love doesn't always need a reply... sometimes it just needs silence.

A Page For You

"How did you like this story?"
    If any one line or one emotion touched your heart...
    Then write here that feeling, which perhaps you did not have words to express:
    ".."
".."
    (Because every reader has his own incomplete story...)

About the Author

Lakhan Agrawal

A boy who writes like this... who sometimes hid behind words, sometimes lived in some name.

"Diary With Your Name" is his first book – a journey, where love did not only mean getting it, it also meant fulfilling it – without saying, without asking.

Lakhan still writes... Shayari, stories, and those emotions that remain alive in the light of pain.

Let's Stay Connected
Instagram: @lakhansoulwrites
Next Book: Coming Soon
"I was just writing, I was just reading"
"If you find yourself in this diary... then you may find
your complete story in the next book."